The Stowaway

Story by Jill McDougall

Illustrations by Wendy Tan Shiau Wei

Contents

Chapter 1

On the Dock

Liverpool, England, 1852

"Get your chestnuts here!" Joseph sang out. "Lovely chestnuts!"

The passengers standing on the Liverpool dock hardly glanced at Joseph. They were busy with their luggage as they prepared to board the sailing ship *Charlotte Jane.* When the tide rose, the great ship would set sail on the four-month voyage to the distant country of Australia.

Joseph smiled sadly to himself. He had not sold a bag of chestnuts all day. But then, he wasn't surprised. The passengers were rich people in fine clothes and Joseph was a twelve-year-old boy in rags.

Nearby, a group of men were speaking in excited voices. It seemed they were off to the goldfields in Australia. One of them, a burly man with fists the size of rocks, noticed Joseph. He strode across the dock towards him.

"Where are you going, Crusher?" called one of the men.

The man they called Crusher didn't answer. His glass-green eyes were fixed on Joseph. "I've hardly got a penny for when I land in the colony," he hissed. "Give me all the money you have, boy."

"Y–yes, sir," stammered Joseph. He reached into his pocket and pulled out his money bag.

"Good lad," said Crusher.

Joseph watched the man lumber up the gangway and onto the ship.

Whew! At least Joseph wouldn't be around when Crusher opened the bag! Crusher would discover nothing inside it except a few spare chestnuts.

Just then, a woman in a green dress hurried towards Joseph. Her arms were full of parcels. A small, pale-faced boy clung to her skirts.

"I'm Mrs McNab," the woman told Joseph. "I'm a passenger on the *Charlotte Jane*."

"And I'm Malcolm McNab," said the little boy in a serious voice.

Joseph smiled at Malcolm and tipped his cap. "Pleased to meet you, Master McNab," he said.

Mrs McNab pointed to some luggage on the dock. "I wonder if you would carry my cabin trunk on board?" she said. "The porters are busy. I'll gladly pay you."

Joseph smiled. "Pleased to be of service, ma'am," he said. He took hold of the woman's trunk and followed her and the boy up the gangway.

Chapter 2

Trapped!

Mrs McNab led the way to a large cabin at the back of the ship. Joseph gazed around in astonishment. The room looked as though it belonged in the queen's palace!

"This is one of the first-class cabins," explained Mrs McNab. She handed Joseph a penny, and added, "My husband is already in Victoria and he wanted me to make the long voyage in comfort."

Joseph nodded thoughtfully. "I suppose you'll be going to the gold diggings," he said.

"No," replied Mrs McNab. "My husband has purchased a sheep farm. There is much good land in the colony."

Malcolm tugged at Joseph's sleeve. "We are taking Albie with us," he said, excitedly. "He's my piggy and he has his own pen up on the deck."

Joseph smiled at the thought of Malcolm's pig enjoying a view of the ocean. However, it was getting late, so he tipped his cap politely and left.

Joseph was making his way across the ship's deck when he felt a hand grab his shoulder.

"Not so fast," growled an angry voice. Joseph turned to see the glass-green eyes of the man called Crusher. "You tricked me!" the man snarled.

Joseph felt a wave of terror. There was no telling what the man would do to him. He turned quickly and twisted out of the man's grip. Then he ran!

Desperately, Joseph searched for somewhere to hide. Just ahead was an open hatch that led below the deck. With his heart pounding, Joseph scrambled down a ladder. Then, he dived into a storage locker and snapped the door shut behind him.

The air in the locker stank of mould. Joseph sank back on a coil of rope as he felt the ship rocking gently back and forth. After a while, his eyes grew heavy and he fell into a doze.

Suddenly, Joseph was thrown sideways. Around him, timbers creaked and groaned. The ship was moving out to sea!

Joseph let out a gasp. There was no turning the ship back around. Joseph was on his way to the other side of the world!

Chapter 3

Down Below

A few hours later, Joseph found himself being hauled onto the deck by a sailor who had discovered his hiding place. The captain of the ship strode towards him.

"So, you're a stowaway," said the captain, glaring at Joseph. "I don't like boys trying to take a free trip on my ship."

Joseph blinked in the bright sunlight. "Yes, Captain," he said, meekly. It was no use explaining that he was an *accidental* stowaway.

"Lucky for you, we need an extra pair of hands," growled the captain. "You can work for your ticket to Australia." He turned to the sailor and said, "Take this boy down to steerage. The new constable will find him somewhere to sleep."

Joseph followed the sailor down a ladder to a long, gloomy room far below the upper deck.

This must be steerage, thought Joseph. It looked like a terrible place. Rows of wooden bunks were fixed to either side of the room and the smell of rats hung in the air.

"That's the constable," said the sailor, pointing to a man sitting at a table. Seeing Joseph's puzzled look, the sailor went on. "The captain appoints some of the biggest men as constables. Their job is to keep the passengers in line." He dropped his voice to a whisper. "Look out for this one. He's a brute."

As Joseph drew close to the constable, he saw that the man was eating from a bowl of stew. At that moment, the ship gave a heave and Joseph was sent crashing into the table. The bowl of stew flipped onto the floor.

"You fool!" shouted the constable. He grabbed Joseph's jacket and shook him hard.

There was silence as the two stared at one another. A chill went up Joseph's spine. He was looking into the glass-green eyes of Crusher!

Chapter 4

The Storm

Over the following weeks, Joseph's life was pure misery. Crusher gave him the hardest chores and, at meal times, Joseph had nothing but scraps to eat. He grew pale and thinner than ever.

One morning, Crusher sent Joseph to feed the animals that were kept on the upper deck.

It was a windy day and dark clouds hung low in the sky. The ocean heaved and the ship was beginning to rock. As a storm approached, sailors rushed to reel in the sails.

"All passengers below!" called the first mate.

Joseph was about to scramble down the hatchway when he spotted a small boy at one of the animal pens. It was Malcolm!

Joseph shouted at Malcolm above the wind. "You need to get below!" he yelled. "A storm is coming."

Malcolm looked at him with wide, anxious eyes. "But Albie will get drowned," he said.

Joseph thought quickly. "We'll cover Albie's pen with this canvas," he said, tying some canvas on with a bit of rope. "Now come with me."

As Joseph spoke, the ship plunged into a giant trough. Malcolm shrieked as he was thrown across the deck.

Joseph lunged towards the little boy and grabbed him just as a torrent of water crashed down on them. The ship tilted and they were both dragged across the deck. In a moment, they would be washed into the ocean.

A rope slid by Joseph's face. He grabbed it with one hand and held on tight. Malcolm let out a scream as they were dashed against the railing of the ship.

Suddenly, Joseph felt a strong arm around him and heard the gruff voice of a sailor. "I've got you both," said the voice. "You're safe now."

Chapter 5

First Class

It was warm in Mrs McNab's cabin, especially with warm broth to sip. On the sofa beside Joseph lay Malcom, still recovering from his ordeal.

"You saved my son's life and risked your own," said Mrs McNab, dabbing at her tears. "You have shown true character, Joseph!"

Joseph managed a weak smile. "It was no trouble, ma'am," he said quietly.

Mrs McNab gazed at him for a moment.

"Tell me, Joseph," she said at last, "what will you do when we reach Australia?"

Joseph thought about Mrs McNab's question. He would be both fearful and excited to begin life in a strange land.

"I'm sure I don't know, ma'am," he said, at last. "But I'll work hard and make my way somehow."

Mrs McNab took his hand. "You are to come and live with us on our farm," she said. "You are a brave, kind boy and you will be treated as one of the family."

Joseph's heart swelled with hope. A family! He had not been part of a family since his parents had died of fever two years earlier.

"I'd … I'd like that very much," he said, with tears in his eyes. "But now I must be getting back." He gave a shudder as he remembered the gloom and stench of his quarters in the belly of the ship.

"You are not to go back to steerage, Joseph," said Mrs McNab, firmly. "I've spoken to the captain and you are to travel in first class for the rest of the voyage."

Seeing Joseph's astonished face, she went on, "A young gentleman has died of the measles and you can have his cabin. I have also bought his clothes for you, and they will be boiled clean."

Joseph stared at her, unable to speak.

"You will have your own servant, too," Mrs McNab said, smiling. "Everyone in first class has a steward to serve them. The captain has found a capable man from below decks to look after you."

Just then, there was a sharp knock at the door. "That will be your man," announced Mrs McNab. "Come in," she called.

The door opened and a bulky figure stood in the doorway.

The man took two steps inside the cabin, then stopped and glared when he spied Joseph on the sofa.

Joseph cringed. It was Crusher himself!

"Get out at once," shouted Crusher, waving his fist at Joseph. Turning to Mrs McNab, he said, "I'm very sorry, ma'am. I don't know how that young fool got in here."

"This boy is no fool," said Mrs McNab quietly. "And from now on, you are to address him as Master Joseph."

Chapter 6

Liverpool Lads

Crusher folded his arms and glared at Joseph. They were in Joseph's cabin now, and Crusher had slammed the door behind them.

"Let's understand one another," said Crusher, his voice swelling with fury. "I will not be a servant to the likes of you!"

When Joseph didn't reply, Crusher went on. "You are no better than me," he said. "You lived on the streets of Liverpool and so did I."

He spat out the words, "I'll never treat you like a master. Not ever!"

Joseph stared silently at Crusher for a moment. He could see the fury in his eyes, but he saw something else, too. It was pride. Joseph understood this kind of pride. It was a pride felt by people who survived the harsh life on the streets. Joseph recognised it because he felt it, too.

Ever since his parents had died, Joseph had needed to look after himself. He had been poor and homeless. For two years, Joseph had slept in doorways and worked for pennies to keep himself from starving.

Crusher suddenly seemed to crumple, as if he couldn't hold onto his rage any longer. "I've always been on me own," he told Joseph. "Ever since I was a young lad like you. But I worked hard." He took a deep breath. "I admit, sometimes I pinched things. But I scraped up enough money for a ticket to Australia." He looked at Joseph. "I've heard all free men are treated equal in the colonies."

Joseph cleared his throat. He felt moved by everything Crusher had said. “You need not be a servant to me,” Joseph said in a solemn voice. “We are both Liverpool lads and Liverpool lads should stick together.”

Then Joseph smiled an apology. “But you might pretend to serve me when we are in Mrs McNab’s company. Otherwise, I fear you’ll be punished.”

Crusher looked thoughtful. “You speak sense, lad,” he said at last. “Mrs McNab would expect me to serve you.” He glanced at the empty jug that sat on the table by Joseph’s bed. “I’ll fetch you some fresh water from the barrel,” he said with a smile.

Chapter 7

Springdale Farm

"It's dinner time!" called Mrs McNab, as the cook carried in steaming plates of mutton and potatoes.

Joseph and Malcolm hurried to the table. They had had a busy morning feeding lambs and collecting eggs from the fowls.

"These boys will make good farmers," said Mr McNab, looking warmly at Joseph.

Joseph smiled contentedly to himself. He was Joseph McNab now, and he was the adopted son of Mr and Mrs McNab of Springdale Farm. It seemed a long time ago that he had stood on the Liverpool dock, dressed in rags.

Joseph's thoughts turned to Crusher. It was strange how things had turned out. If it hadn't been for Crusher, Joseph would never have become an accidental stowaway.

Crusher had lived a hard life, just as Joseph had. On the voyage to Australia, he had told Joseph how his parents had both died of scarlet fever. He had only been a small boy, but somehow he survived the freezing winters on the streets. Now he was hoping to make a new life for himself in a land of sunshine and opportunity.

On the *Charlotte Jane*, Crusher had acted the part of a loyal servant to Joseph. Indeed, he had done so well that he impressed everyone in first class.

"Eat up, Joseph!" said Mrs McNab, interrupting his thoughts. "Have some more potatoes."

Just then there was a knock on the door.

"You may come in, Frederick," called Mrs McNab.

A burly figure entered the dining room. He was carrying a load of wood for the fire. As he placed the logs in the grate, he turned and nodded at Joseph. As he did so, his glass-green eyes shone in the firelight.